FAMOUS
PLACES
UNITED KINGDOM

This edition published in 2004

Grandreams Books Ltd
4 North Parade, Bath BA1 1LF, UK

Designed & packaged by
Q2A Design Studio
Printed in China

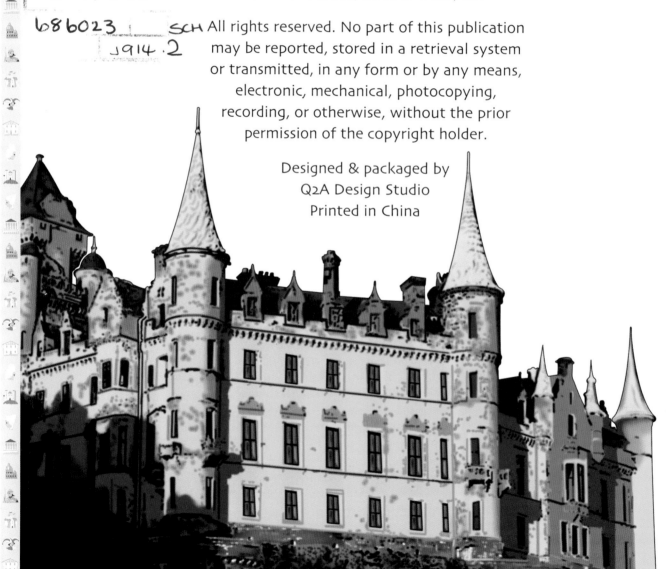

Contents

Which is the oldest restaurant in London?

Rules in Covent Garden is London's oldest restaurant. Started in 1798 by Thomas Rule, it serves traditional English food. There are rooms named after famous people who ate there, such as Charles Dickens, King Edward and Charlie Chaplin.

In whose honour was Boudicca's Statue displayed?

Carved in bronze, Boudicca's Statue was erected in 1850, in London, to honour Boudicca (or Boadicea), the queen of a British tribe called the Iceni. It is said that Boudicca is actually buried at King's Cross Station, beneath track number 10!

Boudicca's Statue

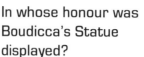

Statue of Eros

Why is the Statue of Eros historic?

The Statue of Eros was the first aluminium statue in London. It was first called the Shaftesbury Monument in honour of the British politician and philosopher, Lord Shaftesbury. The statue stands on top of a bronze fountain.

Where is the largest stone circle in Europe?

The World Heritage site of Avebury in Kennet, England, has the largest stone circle in Europe. It extends more than 400 metres (1,312 feet) in diameter and about 6 metres (20 feet) in height.

Why is Hadrian's Wall unique?

Hadrian's Wall is the only Roman World Heritage site in Britain. At about 118 kilometres (73 miles), it is also the longest of its type in Britain.

What is Discovery Point in Scotland famous for?

Discovery Point in Dundee, Scotland, is the site of the historic ship, RRS Discovery. The ship was the first in Britain to be built specially for scientific research.

What does 'The Cenotaph' signify?

'The Cenotaph' signifies the war memorial erected in London to honour those who lost their lives in World Wars I and II. Sir Edward Lutyens first designed this memorial in 1919. The word cenotaph means 'empty tomb'.

What were the prison cells at Big Ben used for?

The prison cells at the Big Ben clock tower in London were used to lock up members of Parliament who broke the rules of government. The last such instance was recorded in 1880.

What were the Houses of Parliament also known as?

Located by the Thames River, the Houses of Parliament were also known as the Palace of Westminster. The building is said to have over 100 staircases and more than 1,000 rooms! Since 1860, the grounds have included Big Ben, Westminster Hall and the lobbies as well.

What is the Golden Hinde at the River Thames in London?

The Golden Hinde is a full-sized model of Sir Francis Drake's 16th century navy ship by the same name. It was the first British ship to sail the world, between 1577 and 1580. Built during 1971-73, the replica is docked on the Thames River as a museum.

British Parliament

Which game is played annually at the Royal Albert Hall?

The Honda Challenge tennis tournament, one of the most popular indoor tennis events in Britain, is held annually at the Royal Albert Hall in London.

Which museum is known as the 'noisiest museum in the world'?

The Highland Museum of Childhood in Edinburgh, Scotland, is known as the 'noisiest museum in the world.' The first-ever museum to specially focus on the history of childhood, collections include historic games and exhibits on the systems of education and clothes of children from different countries.

Which museum displays different kinds of lawnmowers?

The British Lawnmower Museum in Lancashire, England, houses unusual antique mowers like the Rolls Royce mower, as well as the world's first racing lawnmower.

How did William Shakespeare's original Globe Theatre catch fire?

During the first production of William Shakespeare's play 'Henry VIII' in 1613, gunfire in the first scene set the Globe Theatre's roof on fire. The theatre was destroyed entirely. In 1990, various people donated money to rebuild it.

Globe Theatre

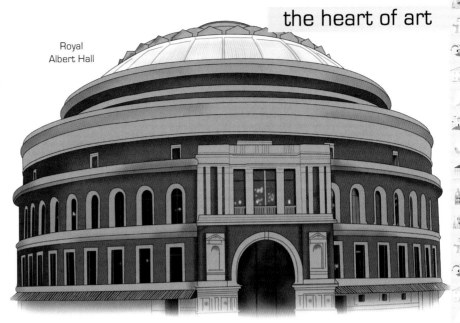

Royal Albert Hall

Where was the Imperial War Museum built?

The Imperial War Museum in London was built on the site of Bethlem Royal Hospital for the mentally ill, also known as Bedlam. The museum, founded in 1917, displays various vehicles and weapons used in war, as well as an art collection.

What historic sale did Christie's make in 1997?

Christie's, the auction house based in London, sold the world's most expensive Mickey Mouse toy in 1997. The toy was a rare Mickey Mouse clock in the shape of a motorcycle. It was sold for $83,650!

Where is the biggest private toy collection in Europe?

The House on the Hill Toy Museum in Essex has the biggest private toy collection in Europe. It includes over 30,000 tin toys, dolls' houses and antique coin-operated machines. The first in the collection was a toy train set bought by the owner in 1946.

Which three historic objects does the National Museum of Photography, Film & Television have?

The National Museum of Photography, Film & Television in Bradford, West Yorkshire, displays the world's first negative (developed film) as well as the first moving picture, and the first-known television recording. It also has the world's largest camera lens.

Why is Tate Gallery so called?

Tate Gallery in London was named after its owner, Sir Henry Tate, who was a sugar manufacturer. This art museum now has two divisions - Tate Britain, with British works, and Tate Modern, which displays the international modern art collection.

Why is the British Museum historic?

The British Museum in London is the oldest museum in the world. The 94 galleries house over 6 million items, the most famous being the Egyptian art collection and the Elgin Marble sculptures of Greece.

on the move

What was the 'Madeleine' experiment carried out by the London Underground?

On March 23, 2001, an air freshener called 'Madeleine' was launched at the St. James Park, Euston and Piccadilly stations to test if the Tube would smell better. This was stopped when the smell was said to be making people sick!

What do the drivers of London Black Cabs have to know, before they are allowed a licence?

London Black Cab drivers must know all the 25,000 streets of the city before they are allowed to drive! The cab service terms this training as 'The Knowledge'.

When was the earliest-known bus service in Britain started?

In July 1829, a 22-seat bus with a door at the back was introduced in Britain by a coach maker. It was pulled along by three horses.

Which is the world's oldest underground railway service?

The London Underground, which began in 1863, is the world's oldest underground railway service. The oldest Tube station is Baker Street, which is famous for its association with the fictional detective, Sherlock Holmes!

Which is the busiest international airport in the world?

London's Heathrow Airport is the world's busiest international airport. On any given day it runs an average of 1,200 flights and transports more than one million passengers every week.

Which is the largest railway station in the United Kingdom?

Waterloo Station in London is the largest railway station in the United Kingdom. The Victory Arch at the station was built in honour of the railway workers who lost their lives during the two world wars.

Where is the world's largest fast ferry?

The Stena HSS in Snowdonia, Wales, is the world's largest fast ferry. Operated by Stena Line Limited, it runs between Holyhead and Dun Laoghaire.

When was London's first modern-day double-decker bus started?

The first fully-covered double-decker bus was launched by the London General Onmibus Company in 1930.

Which airport in London is considered to have the best design?

Stansted Airport is considered to be the best-designed airport in London. It was designed by the British architect, Sir Norman Foster, in 1991.

Stansted Airport

Where can one find the largest collection of American aircraft?

Duxford American Air Museum in England has the largest selection of war planes from World War II. It is also the largest museum of its kind in Europe.

American Air Museum

Which is the oldest school in the United Kingdom?

King's School in Canterbury, England, is said to be the oldest school in the United Kingdom. Famous personalities such as Christopher Marlowe (poet) and David Gower (cricket player) have studied there.

Which boys' public school had the first licensed stained-glass windows in England?

Eton College in Berkshire was, along with Cambridge University, the first to have licensed stained-glass windows in England. John of Utynam, an artist, was given the earliest English patent for making such glass.

Approximately how many schools are there in Great Britain?

There are said to be at least 35,000 schools in Great Britain!

Why is Oxford University considered historic?

Oxford University is the oldest university in the world. Renouned as one of the world's finest institutions for higher studies, the university has been home to such famous people as Margaret Thatcher, Tony Blair and Bill Clinton.

Which college houses the oldest library in Britain?

Merton College at Oxford University houses the oldest library in Britain.

Oxford University

Which famous rock singer studied at the London School of Economics?

Mick Jagger of the music group Rolling Stones graduated from the London School of Economics.

Where can one find Britain's first Internet school?

In August 2000, the Cyber School at Glebe Hall, in Clackmannanshire, Scotland, became Britain's first electronic school. Students there learn with the help of the Internet, instead of teachers.

How was Cambridge University formed?

In 1209, some students of Oxford University moved to Cambridge to escape the violence that had broken out at the city of Oxford. These students then went on to establish Cambridge University.

How many students of London's Imperial College have won the Nobel Prize?

Fourteen students of London's Imperial College have so far won the Nobel Prize. Among them was Sir Alexander Fleming, who invented penicillin - the first antibiotic medicine used to cure infections!

Which is the oldest university in Scotland?

Saint Andrews University, which was established in 1411, is the oldest university in Scotland. It is also the third oldest university in Britain, after Oxford and Cambridge.

Cambridge University

How many LEGO bricks were used to create Legoland Windsor amusement park?

About 32 million LEGO bricks were used to build the Legoland Windsor amusement park. The park also has a Hall of Fame, which displays brick models of famous people like Marilyn Monroe, Winston Churchill and the Queen of England.

What is the Deep Sea World?

The Deep Sea World in Scotland is an aquarium with the world's largest underwater safari tunnel, extending about 112 metres (367 feet) in distance. It also has one of the largest collections of sand tiger sharks in Europe.

What are the popular rides at Alton Towers?

Alton Towers amusement park in Staffordshire, England, offers over 150 rides. These include Oblivion, the world's first roller coaster that drops vertically, and Air, the first 'flying coaster' in Europe.

Why is the London Dungeon unusual?

The London Dungeon is the world's first museum to showcase the history of medieval London's criminals.

Which British centre is based on the history of chocolate?

Cadbury World in Birmingham is the only visitor's centre in Britain that focuses on the history of chocolate.

How did Madame Tussaud's originate?

In 1802, a wax sculptor, Madame Tussaud, began a 33-year-long tour of the British Isles with her wax models of people. When she died, her grandchildren moved the exhibition to London as Madame Tussaud's wax museum.

Where was the world's first reptile house, public aquarium and insect house opened?

London Zoo, which is the world's oldest zoo, opened the first-ever reptile house in 1849. It established the first public aquarium in 1853 and an insect house in 1881. In 1938, it also started a zoo especially for children.

Where can one find Britain's first installed escalator?

Harrods department store in London has Britain's first installed escalator. The escalator was set up in 1878.

Harrods

What is the Megafobia?

The Megafobia, located at Oakwood Coaster Country in Wales, is the biggest wooden roller coaster in Britain.

What is King Arthur's Labyrinth?

King Arthur's Labyrinth in Wales is an underground boat ride that goes through a waterfall into a set of caves. Inside these caves, stories of King Arthur are narrated through sound and light shows.

Which annual tradition is associated with Trafalgar Square?

Since 1947, Trafalgar Square has celebrated Christmas with a tree gifted annually by Norway as a mark of gratitude for Britain's help during World War II.

Which is the largest freshwater lake in Britain?

Loch Lomond in Scotland is the largest freshwater lake in Britain. The lake has about 20 different species of fish, more than in any other British lake.

What is the historic significance of the Shambles?

The Shambles in York is England's oldest medieval street. It was there that the town butchers used to sell meat. The name was derived from the word 'Shamel', meaning the benches on which meat was displayed.

What is Baker Street most famous for?

The address of house number 221B on Baker Street, London, belonged to the famous fictional detective, Sherlock Holmes, and his faithful assistant, Dr. Watson. The house is now the Sherlock Holmes Museum.

Trafalgar Square

Approximately how many shops does Oxford Street have?

Oxford Street in London is said to have over 300 stores! HMV Records at 363 Oxford Street is believed to be the oldest record shop in the world.

What is the legend of Nessie?

Nessie is the name of the mythical monster at Loch Ness, which is Scotland's highest freshwater lake. Legend tells of a strange monster that lives inside the lake. The first recorded sighting of Nessie is believed to have been in AD 565.

Which is the oldest royal park in London?

St. James Park is the oldest royal park in London. It was built on the site of a hospital.

Why is Piccadilly Circus so called?

Piccadilly Circus got its name from 'picadil', a 17th century frilly shirt collar created by a dressmaker who lived in the area. Famous for its neon-lit advertisements, the first electrically-lighted board was put up in 1910.

Piccadilly Circus

What is unusual about the Uffington White Horse?

The Uffington White Horse was carved out of grass taken from the upper slopes of Uffington Castle in Oxfordshire, England. The natural chalk that grew under the grass, however, gave the image its white colour. It is the oldest hill figure in Britain - going back to almost 3,000 years.

What is Regent's Park famous for?

Regent's Park in London is famous for its Open Air Theatre. The theatre is Britain's only professional outdoor theatre and also one of the largest, with seats for more than 1,000 people.

architectural wonders

Marble Arch

What is Falkirk Wheel?
Falkirk Wheel in Scotland is the only revolving boat lift in the world. It can lift at least eight boats at a time, transporting them between canals. The wheel was inaugurated in May 2002 by Queen Elizabeth II.

How tall is Falkirk Wheel estimated to be?
Falkirk Wheel is about 35 metres (115 feet) high - as tall as eight double-decker buses lined together!

Which bridge has been described as a 'giant opening eyelid'?
Gateshead Millennium Bridge over the River Tyne in England is the world's first rotating bridge. It turns on both sides of the river to create an arch, or a 'giant eyelid.'

How is Gateshead Millennium Bridge kept clean?
Gateshead Millennium Bridge is fitted with a mechanism by which any piece of trash dropped on it automatically rolls into a trap every time the bridge opens!

Where was New London Bridge shifted to and why?
In the 1960s, the British government sold New London Bridge as it was found unable to bear the weight of traffic. It was shifted to Lake Havasu City in Arizona, USA, where industrialist Robert P. McCulloch bought it for about $2.5 million.

Who built Admiralty Arch, and why?
Sir Aston Webb designed and built Admiralty Arch in 1910-11, in memory of Queen Victoria. Located in London, it is a structure with three arches and iron gates. For a brief period, it was used as a hostel for the homeless.

Which is the world's first bridge to be cast in iron?
Ironbridge in Shropshire, England, is the world's first bridge to be cast in iron. The first iron boat, too, was built there in 1787.

Why was Marble Arch moved from Buckingham Palace?
The Arch was built in 1828 as the chief entrance to Buckingham Palace, but when the Palace was extended in 1851, the Arch was moved to its current site as an entrance to Hyde Park. Various road changes have left the Arch on a traffic island at the end of Oxford Street, surrounded by cars and concrete.

What is unusual about the length of Forth Railway Bridge?
Forth Railway Bridge in Edinburgh, Scotland, is believed to be longer by nearly one metre in the summer.

What makes Tower Bridge different from the other bridges across Thames River?
Out of the 29 bridges across Thames River, Tower Bridge is the only one that can be folded. Apparently, in 1952, a London bus was forced to jump from one hinged lift bridge to theother, when the bridge began to rise with the bus still on it!

Tower Bridge

Which ancient city is known as the 'home of golf'?

St. Andrews in Scotland is known as the 'home of golf.' Golf has been played on the links at St. Andrews Old Course since the 1400s. Besides being the world's oldest course, St. Andrews Links is also Europe's largest golf complex.

What was the Oval before it became a cricket ground?

The Oval used to be a cabbage garden before it became a cricket ground. Located at Kennington, London, the Oval opened as a cricket ground in 1846.

What makes the Wimbledon tennis courts unique?

The Wimbledon tennis courts host the only Grand Slam tennis matches played on natural grass, popularly known as the Wimbledon Championships.

Which stadium is also known as 'the church of football'?

Wembley Stadium in London was first designated as 'the church of football' by the famous football player, Pelé. The stadium was built on the site of a golf course!

At which British school was the game of rugby invented?

The game of rugby is believed to have begun at Rugby School in Warwickshire, England, in 1823. The game was invented accidentally when schoolboy William Webb Ellis picked up the soccer ball and started running with it! The Rugby World Cup trophy is named after Ellis.

What are some of the unique features of the Millennium Stadium?

The Millennium Stadium in Cardiff, Wales, is the only British stadium with a roof that can be drawn or pulled back. It is the tallest building in Wales and can seat about 72,500 people.

How was the pitch at Lord's prepared in the early days?

In the beginning, sheep were used for preparing the pitch at Lord's. They were let out to chew on the grass!

Where in England was the game of tennis invented?

It is believed that the game of tennis was introduced at a Christmas party by a British army officer, Major Walter Clopton Wingfield. The game was played as lawn tennis then.

Which is the world's first artificially frozen ice-skating rink?

Glaciarium in London is the world's first artificially frozen ice-skating rink. It was opened in 1876.

Which is the oldest cricket ground in Britain?

Lord's Cricket Ground, London, is the oldest cricket ground in Britain. It is also widely acknowledged as the 'home of cricket.' The first match played at Lord's was in 1814.

Lord's Cricket Ground

famous facts

Stonehenge

Why is the Diana, Princess of Wales, Memorial Playground based on a 'Peter Pan' theme?

The Diana, Princess of Wales, Memorial Playground is on the site of an earlier playground funded by the 'Peter Pan' author, J.M. Barrie. The playground is part of an approximately 11 kilometre (7 mile) walkway in Kensington Gardens, London, dedicated to the late Princess Diana.

What kind of certificate is given at the Monument in London?

The Monument in London has a 345 step twisted spiral staircase leading up to a platform inside the column. Those who manage to climb all the way up receive a certificate. Built in 1671-77, the Monument was dedicated to the victims of the Great Fire of London in 1666.

London Monument

Where was the writer Ben Jonson buried?

At Westminster Abbey a small stone with the words 'O Rare Ben Jonson" marks the burial place of the famous British playwright and poet. It is believed that Jonson could not afford to pay for a normal burial space and so was buried standing up!

Where in Britain was the first McDonald's restaurant opened?

The first McDonald's fast-food restaurant in Britain was opened in Woolwich, London, in 1974.

What is unusual about the sunrise at Stonehenge?

The sunrise is not usually seen at the Stonehenge site in Wiltshire, England. However, on June 21, the longest day in the year, the sun emerges from behind the Heel Stone located outside the entrance, as if it were balancing on it.

How many glass panes make up each clock dial of Big Ben?

Although each Big Ben dial was widely believed to have comprised 365 glass panes, it is actually made up of 312 panes.

Westminster Abbey

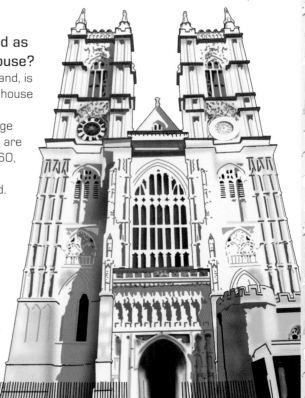

Where is the world's tallest as well as longest garden hedge?

The Meikleour Beech Hedge in Perthshire, Scotland, is the world's tallest and longest garden hedge. Planted in 1746, the hedge is over 500 metres (1,640 feet) long and has an average height of about 30 metres (98 feet). It is trimmed once every 10 years.

Which building is regarded as Britain's most haunted house?

Chingle Hall in Lancashire, England, is regarded as the most haunted house in Britain. The ghosts of monks praying inside the rooms, strange voices, cold chills and footsteps are said to be common. Built in 1260, Chingle Hall is also the oldest existing brick building in England.

Which is the oldest surviving cinema hall in England?

The Electric Cinema in Notting Hill, London, is the oldest surviving cinema hall in England. Founded in 1910, the hall was modernized and reopened in 1993.

Why is Westminster Abbey so called?

The building site of the Westminster Abbey church was originally located several miles to the west of London's city walls, and so it got the name Westminster.

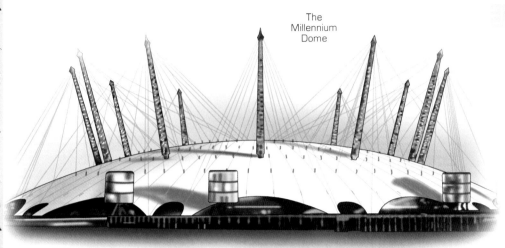
The Millennium Dome

How big is the Millennium Dome?

The Millennium Dome exhibition centre is the largest covered structure in the world. It is believed to be big enough to hold about 18,000 double-decker buses!

Which is Britain's biggest centre for science and astronomy?

The National Space Centre in Leicester, England, is the first, as well as the biggest, exhibition hall for space science. It comprises the Challenger Learning Centre, the first of its kind outside North America, where children can pretend to be astronauts at a space station.

Which attraction in England is the world's largest observation wheel?

The London Eye is the world's largest observation wheel. It looks like a giant bicycle wheel and offers a view of London City from its 32 capsules. It is said to weigh more than 250 double-decker buses!

Where is the world's first inventor centre?

The Big Idea in Irvine, Scotland, is the world's first centre dedicated to the history of inventions. It has a laboratory filled with activities to try out, exhibitions on great inventions and free inventor kits for visitors.

Where can one find Britain's first inflatable restaurant?

Britain's first inflatable restaurant, called O2, can be found at Magna, the country's first science adventure centre located in South Yorkshire. The restaurant is inside a hot-air balloon!

What is the BFI London IMAX Theatre best known for?

The BFI London IMAX Theatre has the largest cinema screen in Britain. The screen is considered to be taller than a 10-storey building!

What kind of attractions does Cairngorm Mountain Limited have?

Cairngorm Mountain Limited in Scotland has exhibition halls, a mountain railway, a reindeer centre and restaurants. The railway line is Scotland's first high-speed cable railway, and the highest of its kind in the world.

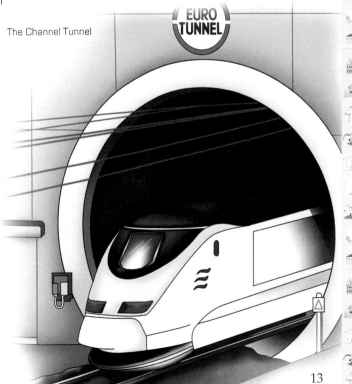
The Channel Tunnel

What is the Millennium Mile?

The Millennium Mile is the name given to the route along the River Thames. It offers views of St. Paul's Cathedral, the Houses of Parliament, Tower Bridge and William Shakespeare's Globe Theatre. The Millennium Mile actually measures about three kilometres (1.86 miles)!

What is the Channel Tunnel?

The Channel Tunnel is the longest underwater tunnel in the world, connecting England to France.

Which is the world's largest greenhouse?

The Eden Project in Cornwall, England, is the largest greenhouse in the world. Built inside an approximately 50 metre (164 foot) pit, it has coffee and rubber plantations, fruits and flowers.

pioneering palaces

Why was Buckingham Palace partly opened to the public in 1962?
In 1962, the Queen's Gallery at Buckingham Palace was opened to show art works from the Royal Collection.

Why is Scone Palace in Scotland famous?
The gardens at Scone Palace are famous for a rare species of pine tree grown there.

Who was the first woman to lead the Queen's Guard at Buckingham Palace?
In July 2000, Captain Cynthia Anderson became the first woman to lead the Queen's Guard at Buckingham Palace.

Buckingham Palace

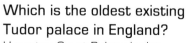

Which is the oldest palace in Europe?
The Tower of London is the oldest palace and fortress prison in Europe.

What is the Ceremony of the Keys?
The Ceremony of the Keys is the daily ritual of locking up the Tower of London. One of the oldest ceremonies of its kind, it has been carried out every night for the last 700 years!

Which is the oldest existing Tudor palace in England?
Hampton Court Palace is the oldest existing Tudor palace in England. The Tudor style of building was based on old English farmhouses.

Which palace once had the longest moat in England?
Fulham Palace, which used to be the official residence of the bishops of London, had the longest moat in England till the early 20th century when it was filled in.

What are the 'Treasure Houses of England'?
The 'Treasure Houses of England' are 10 of the best palaces, houses and castles in the country. They are Castle Howard, Chatsworth, Harewood House, Longleat House, Warwick Castle, Wilton House, Woburn Abbey, Leeds Castle, Beaulieu and Blenheim Palace.

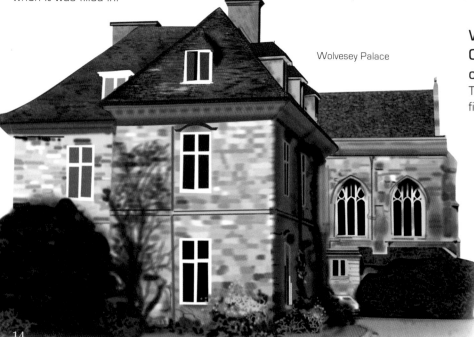

Wolvesey Palace

When was the Queen's Christmas speech first covered on television?
The Queen's Christmas speech was first covered on television in 1957.

How are Wolvesey Palace and Wolvesey Castle different from each other?
Wolvesey Castle was the old home of the Bishop of Winchester. In 1927, it was rebuilt as Wolvesey Palace, which serves as the present house of the Bishop.

Igtham Mote

What is the historic importance of Ightham Mote?

Ightham Mote in Kent is regarded as one of England's finest medieval moated houses (houses surrounded by water-filled ditches). The National Trust, which maintains and conserves buildings, has started a project to repair the 14th century house.

Where can one find the largest fireplace in England?

The entrance hall at Shute Barton Manor House in Devon is considered to have England's biggest fireplace. It is about 6.7 metres (22 feet) wide.

How is Chastleton House connected to sport?

Chastleton House in England is believed to be the place where the rules for the game of croquet were first written in 1865.

What makes New Hall special?

The 12th century New Hall in Birmingham is reputed to be the oldest inhabited moated manor house in England. It has now been converted into a hotel.

What is unique about Hamilton Palace?

Hamilton Palace in Sussex is said to be the most expensive private house built in Britain in the last century. Only partly built, its construction began in 1985 but stopped when the owner, Nicholas van Hoogstraten, was found guilty of killing a business competitor.

Which is the largest private house in England?

Knole House in Kent is the largest private house in England. It is also called the 'calendar house', because of its 365 rooms (for 365 days of the year), 52 staircases (for the weeks of the year) and 7 courtyards (for the days of the week)!

10 Downing Street

Which historic residence did Sir George Downing build?

Sir George Downing built the famous No.10 Downing Street, the official home for British prime ministers since 1732.

In which year was the first stately home in Britain opened to the public?

In 1949, Longleat House in Wiltshire, England, became the first British stately home to open its doors to the public. The maze there is the world's longest and takes about 90 minutes to go through!

Longleat House

How did Owlpen Manor get its name?

Owlpen Manor in Gloucestershire is said to be named after Olla, a Saxon chief who built his 'pen' (staying place) at the site during the 9th century.

What is special about Chedworth Roman Villa?

Chedworth Roman Villa is one of the largest ruins of a Roman villa in England.

15

homes and palaces of england

Which famous discovery was made at Bowood House in Wiltshire?
In 1774, the English chemist, Dr. Joseph Priestley, discovered oxygen at Bowood House's laboratory.

Bowood House

Where is the largest gallery in England?
The Long Gallery at Montacute House, in Somerset, is the largest existing gallery in England. It measures about 52.4 metres (172 feet).

Whose ghost is said to haunt Claydon House?
A grey figure, said to be the ghost of Florence Nightingale has reportedly been seen staring out of the window of the Rose Room of Claydon House, located in Buckinghamshire.

Which animal inhabits the park at Petworth House?
The park at Petworth House has the largest herd of fallow deer in England.

What kind of park surrounds Charlecote House?
Charlecote House in Warwickshire has an ancient deer park around it. The playwright, William Shakespeare, supposedly hunted there.

What makes the stately Spencer House an important landmark?
Spencer House is reputed to be the only great 18th century private palace left intact in London. It was built during 1756-66 for the ancestors of Diana, Princess of Wales.

What is unique about Beningbrough Hall?
The 18th century house of Beningbrough Hall in York has a xentral corridor running along its full length.

Where was the film 'Sense and Sensibility' shot?
The film 'Sense and Sensibility' was partly shot at Wilton House. The 450-year-old house is the home of the Earl of Pembroke.

What makes the gardens of Kinnerseley Castle special?
The gardens of Kinnerseley Castle in Herefordshire have one of the largest ginkgo trees in the United Kingdom. The ginkgo is an ancient and rare tree, with fan-shaped leaves and yellow flowers.

Palladian Bridge at Wilton House

What is Petworth House most famous for?
Petworth House in West Sussex has the largest and best collection of paintings and ancient sculpture maintained by the National Trust, one of Britain's main conservation organizations.

What is unique about the 'Smallest House'?

The 'Smallest House' located in Conwy, Wales, is actually Britain's smallest house! It is about 3 metres (9.8 feet) high and only 1.8 metres (5.9 feet) wide!

Which palace was a favourite country home for the bishops of St. David's?

Bishop's Palace was especially built by the bishops of St. David's as a country home. It had fish ponds, fruit orchards and a deer park.

Which historic home has a 3,000-year-old mummy?

Bodrhyddan Hall in Denbighshire has a 3,000-year-old Egyptian mummy on display. It was brought from Egypt in the 19th century.

Which annual festival is held at Tredegar House?

The Folk Festival is held every May at Tredegar House in Newport. The festival was started in order to celebrate the different forms of folk dance and music practised in South Wales.

Why was the orangery at Margam Castle built?

The orangery (a type of greenhouse) at Margam Castle was built during 1787-93 to house different species of orange and lemon trees. The approximately 99.6 metre (327 feet) long garden is the first indoor orangery in the United King-dom and is also Britain's largest.

What is special about the dining room at Plas Newydd?

The dining room at 18th century Plas Newydd in North Wales has the largest wall painting done by Rex Whistler, a famous 20th century artist. It is 17.67 metres (58 feet) long.

Plas Newydd

What is the meaning of Plas Mawr?

Built in 1576-85, Plas Mawr means the 'Great Hall.' Located in Conwy, it is considered to be one of the best-preserved British town houses from the Elizabethan era.

What are the historic attractions at Margam Castle?

The park around which Margam Castle, was built in the 1830s has the largest hedge maze in Europe.

Which palace used to be the largest in Wales?

St. David's Bishop Palace, built by Henry de Gower during 1328-47, was the largest Welsh palace before it was ruined.

Which famous person was born at Ty Mawr?

Bishop William Morgan, the first-translator of the complete Bible into Welsh, was born at Ty Mawr in 1545.

Margam Castle

homes and palaces of scotland

Which Hollywood film was shot at Hatfield House?
In 2000, the film 'Tomb Raider' was shot at Hatfield House in Hertfordshire. The house is considered to be one of the finest Jacobean-style houses in England.

Hatfield House

Which house was used as a hospital during World War II?
Haddo House near Aberdeen was used as a maternity hospital during World War II. The house belongs to the marquesses of Aberdeen.

Why was Duff House sold?
In the late 19th century, the owners had to sell Duff House due to financial problems. The house in Banff was, by turn, converted into a hotel, a sanatorium and, finally, a public gallery in 1995.

What is special about Paxton House?
The picture gallery at Paxton House in Berwick-upon-Tweed is the biggest in a Scottish country house. It displays more than 70 paintings from the National Galleries of Scotland.

What makes Argyll's Lodging an important Scottish landmark?
Argyll's Lodging is held to be one of the finest surviving 17th century town houses in Scotland. It was the home of the Dukes of Argyll.

What famous collection is on display at Manderston House?
The largest private collection of Blue John, a rare stone, can be seen at Manderston House. The stone is found only in Derbyshire, England.

What is unusual about Winton House?
Winton House in Pencaitland, near Edinburgh, has carved twisted chimneys of stone!

Which house is known as Scotland's 'finest stately home'?
Hopetoun House in Fife is known as Scotland's 'finest stately home.' It was built in the 17th-18th centuries.

Abbotsford House

To which famous personality did Abbotsford House belong?
Abbotsford House in Melrose was the home of the famous Scottish writer, Sir Walter Scott. He built it in 1822, on the site of an old farmhouse.

Why is Abbot House important to Scottish history?
Abbot House in Fife is the only abbot's residence left in Scotland.

Hampton Court Palace

Which palace houses a gallery of cartoon sketches?

The Cartoon Gallery at Hampton Court Palace in London originally displayed Raphael's 16th century cartoons of the 'Acts of the Apostles.' After Queen Victoria gave the cartoons to the Victoria and Albert Museum, the gallery had copies of them painted in 1697.

Where were the first recorded Parliament sessions of Scotland held?

The first recorded Parliament sessions of Scotland were held at Scone Palace in Perth.

How were the Fishbourne Roman Palace ruins found?

Fishbourne Roman Palace was discovered by accident in 1960, when the ground was being dug for a water trench. Later excavations showed that the palace was the site of a military base in AD 43.

On the site of which royal residence was Richmond Palace built?

Richmond Palace in Surrey, England, was built on the site of the 12th century royal home, Sheen.

What is special about Manderston House?

The Georgian-style Manderston House in Duns, Scotland, has a silver staircase, the only one of its kind in the world.

Which famous author was inspired by Groombridge Place?

The gardens of the 17th century Groombridge Place in England inspired the setting for a drama scene in Sir Arthur Conan Doyle's Sherlock Holmes mystery, 'The Valley of Fear.'

Groombridge Palace

Which are the 'Great Houses of Scotland'?

The seven historic homes recognized as the 'Great Houses of Scotland' are Thirlestane Castle, Traquair House, Glamis Castle, Blair Castle, Scone Palace, Ballindalloch Castle and Dunrobin Castle.

What is special about the Royal Tennis Courts at Falkland Palace?

The tennis courts at the 16th century Falkland Palace in Fife, Scotland, are said to be the world's oldest ones in use.

How did Nonsuch Palace get its name?

The 16th century Nonsuch Palace in Surrey, was the last castle to be built by King Henry VIII. He wanted the palace to be unique and, hence, named it 'Nonsuch.'

Who used to live at Bateman's House?

Bateman's in England was the home of author Rudyard Kipling from 1902-1936. His Rolls-Royce can still be seen in the garage of the 17th century house.

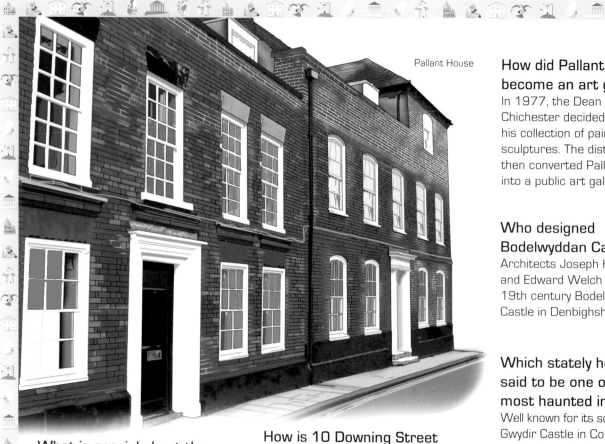

Pallant House

How did Pallant House become an art gallery?

In 1977, the Dean of Chichester decided to display his collection of paintings and sculptures. The district council then converted Pallant House into a public art gallery.

Who designed Bodelwyddan Castle?

Architects Joseph Hansom, and Edward Welch designed 19th century Bodelwyddan Castle in Denbighshire.

Which stately house is said to be one of the most haunted in Wales?

Well known for its so-called ghosts, Gwydir Castle in Conwy has the reputation of being one of the most haunted houses in Wales.

What is special about the Mount Stuart home?

Mount Stuart was the first house in Scotland to have electricity and the first in Britain to have a heated swimming pool.

How is 10 Downing Street in London designed?

The official residence of the British prime minister is actually two houses joint together by a corridor.

Who was the first pop singer to perform at Buckingham Palace?

In May 2002, Sir Elton John recorded a song for the Queen's golden jubilee concert, to become the first pop singer to perform at Buckingham Palace.

What was Maxwelton House originally called?

Built in 1370, Maxwelton House was originally called Glencairn Castle.

Which members of the British royal family are buried at Frogmore House?

Queen Victoria and her husband Prince Albert are buried at a special building in the gardens at Frogmore House.

How did the gardens of Fulham House become famous?

In the 17th century, Bishop Compton started to grow rare flowers (like magnolias) at the gardens of Fulham House. The gardens became the first in Europe to have these flowers.

What is the oldest raven at the Tower of London called?

The name of the 25-year-old raven at the Tower of London is Hardey, who recently completed 21 years there. At a special celebration at the White Tower, Hardey was presented with a sheep's heart!

Tower of London

What are the attractions at Kenwood House?

Kenwood House in London has a library with a curved, painted ceiling. During summers, the house holds open-air concerts by the lake.

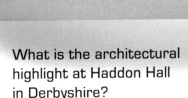

Kenwood House

Which famous house does not stand completely straight?

10 Downing Street leans a little forward onto the street because of its wooden base. In the 1960s, the structure was modified to make it safer.

What do conservation and restoration of architecture mean?

Conservation and restoration of architecture are, respectively, ways of preserving and repairing old and important buildings.

What is the architectural highlight at Haddon Hall in Derbyshire?

The huge, semi-circular steps at Haddon Hall were supposedly made from the roots of a single oak tree.

How was Kew Palace built?

A style of brickwork called Flemish Bond was used to build the four-storeyed Kew Palace in Surrey. Built in the 17th century, it was one of England's first buildings in this style.

What was the cost of restoring the Royal Pavilion?

More than £10 million was spent to restore the Royal Pavilion palace in Brighton! The restoration began in 1982 and lasted for about 10 years.

Which stately home is said to have the 'finest medieval hall in England'?

The Baron's Hall at 14th century Penhurst Place in Kent is regarded as the oldest and finest medieval hall in England.

How was money raised for the restoration of Longleat House?

In 2002, officials of Longleat House auctioned rare books and artworks from the house's collection. These included the first-ever printed book in the English language. Over £27 million was collected in this way.

What unique feature does Tatton Park have?

Tatton Park in Cheshire, England, has a railway in its basement for the transportation of coal!

What is unusual about the design plan of Ickworth House?

18th century Ickworth House in Suffolk has an oval shape and curved corridors.

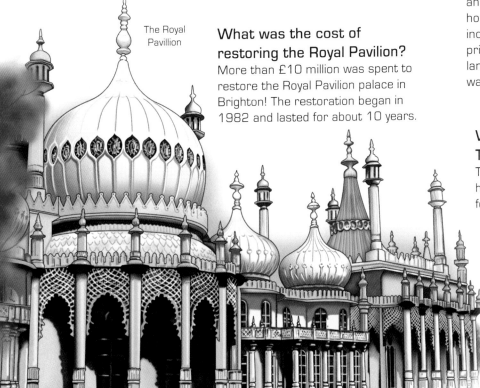

The Royal Pavillion

sights to see

What is unusual about the gardens at Hall Place?
The gardens at Hall Place in Kent include a herb garden especially designed for blind people. It labels the herbs in Braille, a method of printing that helps the blind to read letters and numbers.

What is special about the garden at Kingston Lacy Palace?
The garden at Kingston Lacy Palace in Dorset has four pink-coloured obelisks (four-sided pillars) that were transported all the way from an Egyptian temple.

Kingston Lacy Palace

What is special about the Fountain Court at Somerset House?
The Edmond J. Safra Fountain Court at Somerset House was the first important public fountain to be designed in London after the year 1845.

Which historic home has a laundry dating back to the Victorian era?
Beningbrough Hall has a fully-furnished Victorian laundry that shows how servants in the Victorian era washed clothes.

Which modern facility has been provided to the Royal Mews staff?
The Royal Mews staff has access to e-mail and the Internet, whereby they can communicate with Buckingham Palace.

Which stately house holds weddings inside its stables?
Harewood House in Yorkshire holds wedding functions in its Courtyard Suite, the converted 18th century stable block.

What are the Royal Mews?
The Royal Mews are the working stables at Buckingham Palace. The Royal Household department there provides horse-drawn carriages and motor cars for members of the royal family.

Which stately home is famous for its art collection?
Wilton House in Salisbury, England, possesses a wide collection of famous Van Dyck paintings.

Where is the Royal Ceremonial Dress Collection?
The Royal Ceremonial Dress Collection can be seen at Kensington Palace in London. It includes clothes and other items dating back to the 18th century.

Which sport is Goodwood House in Sussex England associated with?
In 1727, the Duke of Richmond, who owned Goodwood House, is said to have participated in the match played with the first ever rules of cricket. In fact, the first match was recorded even earlier, in 1702.

Kensington Palace

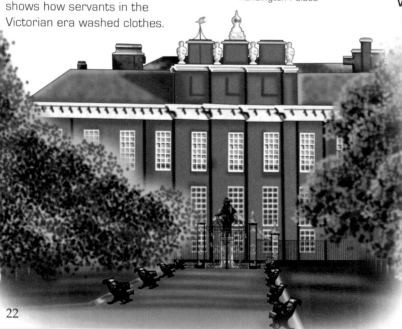

Linlithgow Palace

Which is the official home of the Archbishop of Canterbury?

Lambeth Palace in London has been home to the Archbishop of Canterbury since about the start of the 13th century.

Which famous scientist was born at Woolsthorpe Manor?

Sir Isaac Newton was born at Woolsthorpe Manor in Lincolnshire. The old apple tree in the orchard of the 17th century house is believed to have been grown from the same tree which led Newton to discover the Law of Gravity.

Who was born at Linlithgow Palace?

On December 8, 1542, Mary, Queen of Scots, was born at Linlithgow Palace.

Where was Charles I born?

Charles I was born at Dunfermline Palace on November 19, 1600. He was the last monarch to be born in Scotland.

When did Buckingham Palace become the official home of the British royal family?

Buckingham Palace became the official London home of the British royal family in 1837, when Queen Victoria first sat on the throne.

Who lies buried at Althorp House in Northamptonshire?

The 16th century Althorp House, built by Sir John Spencer, was both the childhood home and burial ground of Diana, Princess of Wales.

Who lived at Haworth Parsonage?

Haworth Parsonage in Yorkshire was the home of the Brontë sisters, Charlotte, Emily and Anne. They wrote some of the greatest English novels. In 1928, the house was inaugurated as the Brontë Parsonage Museum.

Which famous poet lived at Dove Cottage?

William Wordsworth lived at Dove Cottage during 1799-1808. Earlier, the 17th century home in Grasmere was a guest house called 'Dove and Olive.'

Blenheim Palace

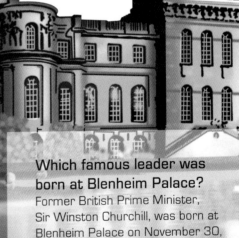

At which historic home was the author of 'Peter Pan' born?

Barrie's Birthplace in Kirriemuir, Scotland is so named in honour of the 'Peter Pan' author, J.M. Barrie, who was born there in 1860.

Which famous leader was born at Blenheim Palace?

Former British Prime Minister, Sir Winston Churchill, was born at Blenheim Palace on November 30, 1874. The 18th century princely home is now a World Heritage site.

23

inside a church

What is a lectern?
A lectern is a stand used in churches for holding the Bible. Many lecterns display a wooden or brass eagle stretching its wings, symbolizing Jesus Christ's return to life after death.

Brass eagle on the Holy Rood Lectern

What were chained libraries?
Many cathedrals had chained libraries in the 17th and 18th centuries. Chaining books in libraries was a common method to enable books to be taken only up to the reading tables, and not outside the library!

A chained book

What is the main area inside a church called?
The nave is the main area inside a church. It is surrounded by aisles and has a seating arrangement in the middle. Naves were so called because they resembled the inside of a ship. The word comes from the Latin 'navis', which means 'ship'.

What were church crypts used for?
A crypt, or a hidden chamber under the floor of a church, was used for hiding, meeting or burying people. The crypt at St. Paul's Cathedral in London is the largest in Europe.

Why were the mural paintings at St. Albans Cathedral undiscovered for a long time?
The 13th century mural paintings at St. Albans Cathedral were hidden under whitewash until 1862. The paintings had been designed by the monks of the cathedral.

Why were the coffins in the crypt at St. Andrews Guild Church removed?
When St. Andrews Guild Church in London was to be converted into a community centre, about 900 coffins were dug out of its ancient crypt. The removal of the coffins cost over £1 million!

What is the Holy Rood Lectern at St. Michael's Church made of?
The Holy Rood Lectern at St. Michael's Church, in Southampton, is made of brass. It was earlier painted brown, which is why it was first thought to be wooden. The lectern dates back to about 1350. It has a triangle-shaped base that supports a brass eagle, with a dragon under its claws.

Why did people stand and pray in churches before the 16th century?
Churches had no place for sitting until the late 1500s. People used to stand in the nave during service. When longer sermons became popular, pews or long wooden benches, were invented.

Which cathedral in England has the longest nave?
The nave in the Cathedral of Saint Albans, in Hertfordshire, is the longest in England. It has a length of about 91 metres (299 feet).

Church Organ

When was the first church organ in England made?
England's first church organ was made in AD 700. Saint Aldhelm, the founder of Malmesbury Abbey in England, built the organ.

How did St. Mary s Church in Suffolk, England, raise money for its repair work?

In January 2003, St. Mary s Church set up an online shopping mall. The church would thereby receive a small amount from all products sold.

How was the spire of the Coventry Cathedral installed?

When St. Michael s Cathedral in Coventry was rebuilt during the late 1950s and the early 1960s, the metal spire was flown in by helicopter! It took about 8 minutes for builders to put the spire in place.

What is the Scientists Corner at Westminster Abbey?

The Scientists Corner at Westminster Abbey marks the burial places of scientists such as Sir Isaac Newton and Charles Darwin.

Who designed St. Paul s Cathedral in London?

The famous British architect Sir Christopher Wren designed St. Paul s Cathedral in London. It is considered to be Wren s most famous design.

What is the Dean s Eye Window?

The 13th century Dean s Eye Window at Lincoln Cathedral is considered to be one of England s finest stained-glass windows. In January 2003, about £200,000 was given to the cathedral for repair work on the window.

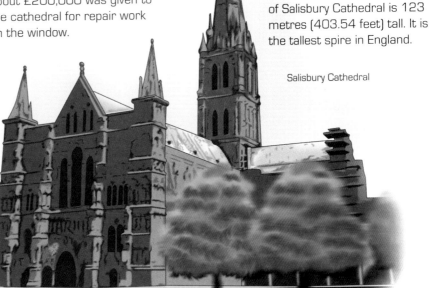

What does the black marble slab in the crypt at St. Paul s Cathedral signify?

The black marble slab in the crypt at St. Paul s Cathedral marks the burial place of Sir Christopher Wren.

How tall is the spire of Salisbury Cathedral?

The spire (a long, pointed structure on top of a building) of Salisbury Cathedral is 123 metres (403.54 feet) tall. It is the tallest spire in England.

Salisbury Cathedral

What do the red public telephone box and the Anglican cathedral in England have in common?

The red public telephone box and the Anglican cathedral in England were both designed by the same architect, Sir Giles Gilbert Scott.

What is the significance of the swan painted on the stained-glass windows at Lincoln Cathedral in England?

It is believed that Saint Hugh, a holy man who helped rebuild Lincoln Cathedral, had a swan that would hiss at anyone who came too close to the saint!

Who designed Rochester Cathedral?

A Norman priest, Bishop Gundulf, designed Rochester Cathedral. The cathedral is the second oldest in England and also houses the country s oldest oil painting, the Wheel of Fortune.

Rochester Cathedral

What is special about Wells Cathedral?

Wells Cathedral in Somerset, England, has the oldest working clock face in the world! The clock itself is the second oldest in England.

What marks out the Scottish Cathedral of the Isles?

The Cathedral of the Isles, or the Scottish Episcopal Church, in Millport, Scotland, is known to be the smallest cathedral in the United Kingdom. It can seat only about 70 people!

Which cathedral has a memorial for coal miners?

In 1947, a memorial was set up at Durham Cathedral to honour both living and dead coal miners.

Durham Cathedral

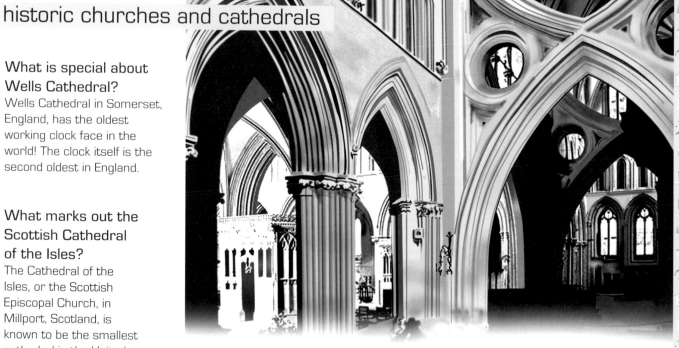

Wells Cathedral

Which cathedral has the world s oldest mechanical clock?

The mechanical clock at Salisbury Cathedral in England is more than 600 years old!

What makes Oxford Cathedral special?

Oxford Cathedral is the only church that serves as a cathedral as well as a college chapel.

Which is the largest cathedral in England?

St. Paul s Cathedral, London, is the largest cathedral in England.

What was significant about the choir which performed at Winchester Cathedral in 1999?

In 1999, Winchester Cathedral in England had an all-girls choir performing for the first time in 900 years.

Where can one find the heaviest set of bells in the world?

Liverpool Cathedral in England has 13 bells that weigh more than 84,000 kilograms.

What is special about Hereford Cathedral?

Hereford Cathedral in England has the largest chained library in the world. It houses more than 1,500 books dating back to the 8th century.

Why is Exeter Cathedral considered unique?

Exeter Cathedral in Devon, England, has the world s longest stone vault (an arched ceiling of a church).

Which cathedral has the largest bell in Britain?

The bell at St. Paul s Cathedral is the largest in Britain. Known as Great Paul, it weighs about 17,000 kilograms (37,478 pounds).

St. Pauls Cathedral

Which Bible is made of calf skin?

The Winchester Bible, produced at Winchester Cathedral during the 12th century, is made of calf skin. It is decorated with gold leaves and gemstones brought from Afghanistan. The Bible took 20 years to complete.

Which cathedral in England was also used as a prison, a bakery and a pigsty?

Southwark Cathedral in London was rebuilt in the 13th century after a fire destroyed the original church in 1212. Since then, some sections of the cathedral have been used as a prison, a bakery and even as a pigsty!

Whose portrait can be seen at the Great Hall of Christ Church Cathedral?

The Great Hall of Christ Church Cathedral in Oxford displays the portrait of Alice Liddell, the inspiration behind the lead character in Alice in Wonderland. It is believed that in damp weather the face of the ghost of Dean Liddell, who was Alice s father, appears on the wall at the cathedral s south aisle!

What kind of a church is Bristol Cathedral?

Bristol Cathedral is a hall church. This is a unique form of church where the ceiling, or roof, extends across the same height, making the church look like one single hall.

Bristol Cathedral

To whom is the Teaching Window at Lincoln Cathedral dedicated?

The Teaching Window at Lincoln Cathedral is dedicated to George Boole, the English mathematician who helped in the development of computers.

What is special about the tower at Derby Cathedral?

The tower at Derby Cathedral stands over 64 metres (210 feet) tall and is held to be the second highest in England. It also has the oldest ring of 10 bells in the world.

Who was killed at Canterbury Cathedral?

Thomas Becket, the archbishop of Canterbury, was murdered on December 29, 1170, at Canterbury Cathedral.

What is special about Manchester Cathedral?

Manchester Cathedral in England is the only one to have a mixed choir, comprising both boys and girls.

Which was the first church in England to have electric lights?

St. Anne s Church in Staffordshire was the first church in England to be lit by electricity.

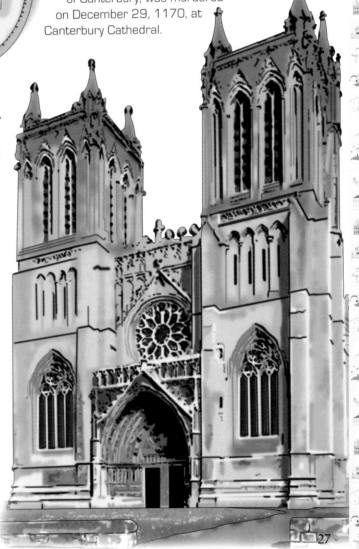

Which cathedral has the tallest spire in Yorkshire?

Wakefield Cathedral has the tallest spire in Yorkshire, England s historic county. It is about 75 metres (246 feet) tall.

What is the connection between Alice in Wonderland and Ripon Cathedral?

The carvings of beasts at Ripon Cathedral is said to have inspired Lewis Carroll to create certain characters and scenes in his novel, Alice in Wonderland .

Coventry Cathedral

What was the original Cross of Nails?

The original Cross of Nails at Coventry Cathedral was made by a local priest, the Reverend Arthur Wales, from three medieval nails. The cross is generally regarded as a symbol of understanding and harmony.

Where is the sculpture of St. Michael and the Devil?

The famous bronze sculpture of St. Michael and the Devil can be seen at Coventry Cathedral. St. Michael is regarded as one of God s favourite angels who led the heavenly forces to victory against Lucifer, the Devil. Sir Jacob Epstein created the sculpture in 1958.

Whose grave lies at Winchester Cathedral?

The grave of Saint Swithun, who lived during the 9th century, lies at Winchester Cathedral. After he died, his bones were thought to heal the sick!

Winchester Cathedral

Where can one find the oldest piece of English embroidery?

Durham Cathedral is said to house England s oldest existing piece of embroidery - a 10th century scarf.

Who holds the record for having played the organ at every cathedral in England?

Christopher Nixon, a 26-year-old primary school teacher, holds the record for having played the organ at every cathedral in England.

Which is the largest Anglican cathedral in Britain?

Liverpool Cathedral is the largest Anglican cathedral in Britain. It is also the fifth largest cathedral in the world.

Which abbey in England is also a national sports centre?

Bisham Abbey in Buckinghamshire has been a national sports centre for the past 50 years.

Where was William Shakespeare baptized?

William Shakespeare was baptized at Holy Trinity Church in Stratford-Upon-Avon, England, in 1564. He was buried in the same church in 1616.

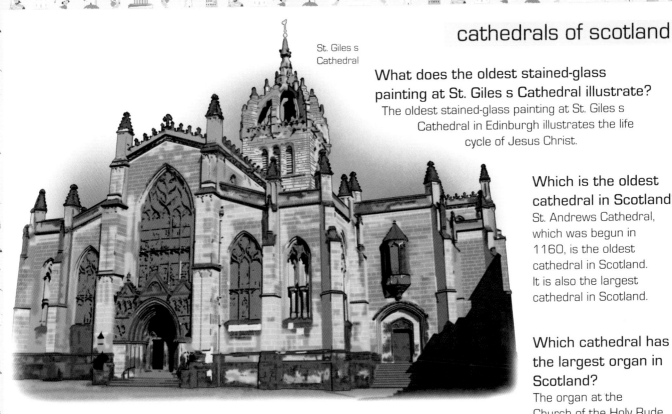

St. Giles s Cathedral

Glasgow Cathedral

What does the oldest stained-glass painting at St. Giles s Cathedral illustrate?

The oldest stained-glass painting at St. Giles s Cathedral in Edinburgh illustrates the life cycle of Jesus Christ.

Which is the oldest cathedral in Scotland?

St. Andrews Cathedral, which was begun in 1160, is the oldest cathedral in Scotland. It is also the largest cathedral in Scotland.

Which cathedral has the largest organ in Scotland?

The organ at the Church of the Holy Rude (Holy Cross) in Stirling has 4,297 pipes and is the largest of its kind in Scotland.

What is special about St. Mary s Church?

St. Mary s Church in Saint Andrews was the earliest collegiate church in Scotland.

Which Scottish cathedral has a museum of religion and art?

Glasgow Cathedral houses St. Mungo s Museum of Religious Life and Art, which is the first museum in the United Kingdom to be dedicated to religion. It was opened in 1993.

How did Sweetheart Abbey get its name?

Sweetheart Abbey in Dumfries was so called in honour of a countess called Lady Devorgilla. In 1273, she dedicated an abbey to her dead husband. It is said that she had his heart preserved and placed in a silver-and-ivory casket, constantly carrying it with her until her death. The abbey was renamed Sweetheart after she was buried there.

Who built the Italian Chapel in Orkney?

The Italian prisoners of World War II made the Italian Chapel in Orkney. They were devout Catholics who built the chapel because there was none at their camp.

What was the first Christian church in Scotland called?

The first Christian church in Scotland can be found at Whithorn and was called Candida Casa (White House).

Why is the Apprentice Pillar at Rosslyn Chapel so called?

The Apprentice Pillar at Rosslyn Chapel, near Edinburgh, got its name from the belief that in the absence of the master mason, the pillar was completed by his apprentice (student). The beauty of the pillar made the mason so jealous that he killed the apprentice!

What is unusual about the bell-ringing style at St. Magnus Cathedral?

The bells at St. Magnus Cathedral in the Orkney Islands use clocking , a Norwegian style of bell-ringing. The bell-ringer works the bells either by hand or by using foot pedals.

cathedrals of wales

Which Welsh cathedral was named after a nobleman who dreamt of a white ox?

St. Woolos Cathedral in Newport was named after Gwynllyw, the fifth century lord of Gwynllwg. According to legend, he had a dream about finding a white ox with a black spot on a nearby hill. When the dream came true, he adopted the Christian religion!

What legend surrounds a saint who was buried at Llandaff Cathedral?

When the bones of Saint Dyfrig were dug up at Llandaff Cathedral, the monks there washed them with water. Legend has it that the water bubbled as if something extremely hot was thrown into it!

How was Llandaff Cathedral destroyed?

Much of Llandaff Cathedral was destroyed in 1941 when a German mine blew up near it. The cathedral was first built in the 12th century.

Why is Bangor Cathedral so called?

Bangor in Welsh means a fence made of sticks. Bangor Cathedral got its name from a similar type of fence it had in the sixth century.

How did the founder of Llandaff Cathedral become famous after his death?

St. Teilo, the founder of Llandaff Cathedral, died in the sixth century AD. However, when his coffin was dug up in 1736, the body was found wrapped in leather and undamaged!

Which is the largest cathedral in Wales?

St. David s Cathedral in Pembrokeshire is the largest cathedral in Wales.

Which object at Brecon Cathedral was said to have healing powers?

The Brecon Cross, or the Crog Aberhonddu, was said to have mysterious healing powers. This belief made the cathedral an important pilgrimage centre during the medieval period.

What was the popular belief about the well at St. Govan s Chapel?

The water in the well at St. Govan s Chapel was believed to heal various illnesses related to the eyes and the bones.

Where is the first Welsh translator of the Bible buried?

Bishop William Morgan, who was the first to translate the Bible into the Welsh language, lies buried at St. Asaph Cathedral in Denbighshire.

Why is St. Margaret s Church also known as the Marble Church ?

St. Margaret s Church in Wales is also known as the Marble Church because fourteen different types of marble were used in the structure.

St. David s Cathedral

Malmesbury Abbey

What happened to the spire at Malmesbury Abbey?

The central spire at Malmesbury Abbey in Wiltshire fell down in a storm, sometime during the 15th or 16th century. It was once higher than even the one at Salisbury Cathedral.

Whose heart was found at Melrose Abbey?

In 1996, the heart of Robert the Bruce, the King of Scotland during 1306-29, was found in a casket at Melrose Abbey in Scotland.

What is the popular belief associated with Bath Abbey?

In 1137, a fire had destroyed the original abbey. It is believed that Bishop Oliver King, secretary to King Henry the Seventh, built Bath Abbey after he heard a voice in his dreams saying, Let a king restore the church. Soon after, the bishop rebuilt the Norman abbey church and named it the Bath Abbey.

Which abbey in England is known for making honey and wine?

Buckfast Abbey in Devon is famous for its honey and wine. The Buckfast Tonic Wine is said to have a secret formula of its own!

Where was the Stone of Destiny found after it had been stolen?

Stolen from Westminster Abbey on December 25, 1950, the Stone of Destiny mysteriously turned up at the altar of Arbroath Abbey in Scotland, in April 1951!

In what way is Netley Abbey in Southampton, England, believed to be haunted?

The ghost of a monk is said to haunt Netley Abbey during Halloween, and also stand guard over a mysterious treasure in the abbey s secret tunnel.

What is unusual about the burial of David Livingston?

The body of the famous Scottish explorer, David Livingston, was buried at Westminster Abbey, while his heart was buried in Tanzania, Africa!

Who were the White Monks at Tintern Abbey?

The monks at Tintern Abbey in Monmouthshire, Wales, were called the White Monks because they only wore white-coloured woollen clothes!

Which abbey is the burial place of Sir Walter Scott?

Sir Walter Scott, a famous Scottish writer, was buried at Dryburgh Abbey in Scotland.

Dryburgh Cathedral

Who is said to haunt Thornton Abbey, near Cleethorpes?

Sir Thomas de Grethem, who was walled alive in Thornton Abbey s secret chamber, is said to haunt the place. His skeleton was supposedly found at a desk at the abbey in the 1830s, with a book and pen in its hands!

interesting facts

Which cathedral produces its own variety of beer?

Chester Cathedral in England has been producing its own variety of beer for the last 1,000 years! It is called Chester Pilgrim Ale.

What is the legend of the witch dance performed at St. Andrews Church in 1590?

It is believed that during the Halloween of 1590, witches danced around St. Andrews Church, in Scotland, to cast evil spells on King James VI!

Where is the first-ever Bible that was printed in English?

The first-ever Bible to be printed in English is housed in the library of Canterbury Cathedral, in England. The library also has a rare world map dating back to 1493.

Canterbury Cathedral

Where can one find the oldest clock in Scotland?

The 16th century tower at St. Brides Church in Douglas has the oldest working town clock in Scotland.

What was the chapel at Bedford Hospital secretly used as?

For five years, the chapel at Bedford Hospital was used as a morgue to house dead bodies, since the one at the hospital was full.

Which English cathedral was featured in Harry Potter and the Philosopher s Stone ?

The 900-year-old Gloucester Cathedral was featured in Harry Potter and the Philosopher s Stone . Later, the cathedral was also used for the filming of the second film in the series, Harry Potter and the Chamber of Secrets.

Which chapel was the first in Britain to accept prayers through e-mail?

In September 2002, Rosslyn Chapel in Scotland started an online prayer service through which people could send prayers and requests by e-mail!

Which famous film was shot at St. Paul s Cathedral?

The film Lawrence of Arabia , made in 1962, was partly shot at St. Paul s Cathedral. It won four Oscar Awards.

What is the popular legend about St. Oran s Chapel in Wales?

It is believed that when St. Oran s Chapel was being built, its walls kept collapsing. Believing this to be the work of evil spirits, the builders buried one of the workers, Oran, alive into the walls in order to satisfy the spirits!

Which is the only cathedral in the British Isles to have a dungeon?

St. Magnus Cathedral in Scotland is the only cathedral in the British Isles with a dungeon. It is known as Marwick s Hole.

St. Magnus Cathedral

Why was a carved figure at Lincoln Cathedral put on ice?

The carved figure of a 600-year-old angel was put in a freezer to kill off the deathwatch beetles growing on the surface!

Why did a rowing team sail across Scotland?

In 2002, a former music teacher and his team sailed from Cumbrae to Edinburgh, to raise money for an organ at the Scottish Episcopal Church. They raised about £35,000.

What is the link between the parish church of St. Mary s and Dracula ?

The graveyard at St. Mary s Church in Whitby, Yorkshire, is said to have inspired the author, Bram Stoker, to write the famous horror story Dracula !

What happened to the medieval statues at Lincoln Cathedral?

It is said that during the 18th century, a person who was repairing the statues at Lincoln Cathedral pulled off the heads of a few male bishop statues. Some of the heads were mistakenly put onto the bodies of female statues!

Why did a priest spend 10 hours on a church rooftop?

In December 2002, the Reverend Bob Thorn stood watching out for Santa Claus from the rooftop of St. Augustine s Church in Hitchurch, England! He did this to raise money for repairing the church s leaking roof.

Lincoln Cathedral

Which abbey s name means Vale of Flowers ?

The name of Strata Florida Abbey, located in Aberystwyth, Wales, means Vale of Flowers. It was once also known as the Westminster Abbey of Wales.

What was the age of the oldest man to be buried at Westminster Abbey?

In 1635, Thomas Parr was buried at Westminster Abbey at the age of 152 years!

When was the electric organ first used in Britain?

In 1898, the organ at Lincoln Cathedral became the first in Britain to be blown by electricity.

How did Christopher Coulthard steal from churches?

Christopher Coulthard robbed the safes and charity boxes of over 500 churches in both Wales and England. He used to dress up as a tourist, carrying his stealing tools in a camera bag! In January 2003, he was sent to prison for four years.

Which cathedral in England is made of trees?

Whipsnade Cathedral in Bedfordshire is a tree cathedral. It is a unique collection of trees arranged in the shape of a cathedral.

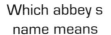

Westminster Abbey

once upon a time...

The 12th century Orford Norman Castle

Which was the first castle built by King William I?
Windsor Castle was the first in a series of nine castles that England's King William I built around London.

How were the earliest castles made?
The earliest castles were made by England s first knights, the Normans, in motte and bailey style. This simple method used earth and wood to build the castle in just a few weeks.

Duke William

From where did the word castle originate?
The word castle originated from the Latin castellum , meaning fortification , or something that strengthens, especially to defend a place against attack. The place could be a fortress, a fort or a castle.

Were there any castle-like structures before the Norman castles?
Before the Norman castles, the Iron Age people of ancient Britain dug hilltops to build huge earthworks for defence. One such is Maiden Castle in Dorset.

What did castles look like before the year 1100?
When we think of castles, we think of stone monuments. However, before the year 1100, castles were wooden structures with thatched roofs, based on a motte and bailey plan of building.

Why did stone castles replace the motte and bailey form?
Compared to the motte and bailey form, stone castles were larger, taller and more reliable for defence purposes. Moreover, the timber and wood used in the earlier form were found to be unsafe in the event of a fire.

What was the licence to crenellate ?
Under Norman rule, noblemen could not build castles without the monarch s permission. Formal authority was granted by a licence to crenellate. The first such licence is said to have been issued for Bishopton Castle in 1143.

For what reasons were castles built?
Castles were originally built as places for noblemen to live in, as military bases and as seats of government. Later structures, which are sometimes called castles, were either forts built for defence or stately homes.

What were concentric castles?
Concentric castles were enclosed castles surrounded by an extra curtain wall, so that the inner walls were higher than the outer ones. Often, these castles were surrounded by water as well. This ensured that any attacker would have had to fight through a series of barriers.

Why was Balmoral Castle rebuilt in 1852?
Scotland s Balmoral Castle was rebuilt in the Scottish Baronial style by Prince Albert. He had bought it as a gift for Queen Victoria, after the death of the original owner.

Balmoral Castle

A stained-glass window at Cardiff Castle

What were castle windows made of?

Glass was expensive and so was rarely used in castle windows. Only smaller windows used glass, which was often decorated with stained-glass paintings. Larger windows used wooden shutters, or other materials such as oiled sheepskin and goatskin. Some window coverings were even made from animal horn.

What were curtain walls?

A curtain wall, or an enclosing wall, of a castle encircled the entire structure and was usually attached to the towers and the gatehouse. The early curtain walls were made from heavy wood.

Why did castles have gatehouses?

Castles had at least one gatehouse to serve as a kind of doorway between two towers to let people in and out. At the same time, a movable drawbridge or a portcullis at the entrance provided protection.

What was the solar in a castle used for?

The lord s private room within the castle was called the solar. Sometimes, when the lady of the castle used the solar, it was called a bower.

What was the privy in a castle?

Privy was the medieval term for bathroom! It was also called the necessarium, jakes, draught or gong. Those who cleaned the privy were known as mudatorlatrinarum, or gong farmers.

Drawbridge

What was an oubliette?

The oubliette was a tiny chamber where prisoners were kept. These early castle prisons were usually in the shape of thin cylinders. The only entrance into the windowless chambers was through a trap door in the ceiling.

Portcullis

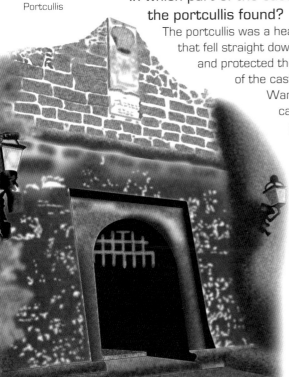

In which part of the castle was the portcullis found?

The portcullis was a heavy, grilled door that fell straight down through slots and protected the main entrance of the castle. Caldicot, Warwick and Hever castles still have portcullises.

What was a lavabo?

A lavabo, or laver, was a stone basin built into the wall of a castle. It served as a wash basin for washing hands before and after eating.

What were the first castle drawbridges like?

Most of the early castle drawbridges were made of wood, and were removable. This meant that guards could easily pull away the platform from its place to safeguard the castle from enemies.

What did the kitchens in early castles look like?

Kitchens in early castles were made of wood and had thatched roofs. A covered path known as the pentice led up to the dining room.

ghouls on the prowl!

Edinburgh Castle

Who haunts Edinburgh Castle?

Edinburgh Castle is located high on a volcanic rock above Princes Street, and right in the centre of the city. The castle is said to house several ghosts, including a drummer who only appears when the castle is about to be attacked!

What kind of a ghost is said to haunt Kenilworth Castle in England?

The ghost of a monk is said to walk the grounds of Kenilworth Castle.

What is the chilling story of Chillingham Castle?

Chillingham Castle is said to have a ghost known as the Blue Boy or the Radiant Boy! The legend started when, in the 1920s, a boy s bones and pieces of a blue dress were found there.

What is strange about Caerphilly Castle?

It is said that the flag tower of Caerphilly Castle in South Wales always smells of perfume!

What eerie incident occured at Jedburgh Castle?

At Scotland s Jedburgh Castle, a creepy ghost was once believed to have been seen in a cloak, which, when pulled away, was empty!

What is the legend behind the ghost at Scotland s Comlongon Castle?

Legend has it that, in 1570, Lady Marion Carruthers jumped off Comlongon Castle s balcony because she did not want to get married. Since then, no grass would grow where she fell and a crying woman s spirit was often seen around.

What makes Glamis Castle unique to ghost hunters?

Known as the most haunted castle in Scotland, Glamis Castle is supposed to house vampires, witches, monsters and ghosts! Strange sounds come from the tower where the castle s owner, Earl Beardie, supposedly challenged the devil to a card game.

Who is said to haunt Craignethan Castle in Lancashire?

Mary, Queen of Scots, spent the night at Craignethan Castle before the Battle of Langside. It is said that her ghost haunts the castle.

What is unique about the ghost at Leeds Castle?

Leeds Castle is believed to be haunted by a big, black dog. It is supposed to bring bad luck. However, there is a story that the ghost once saved a woman s life. The woman, on seeing the ghost, jumped away from the window where she was sitting, just before the wall supporting it fell!

What is strange about the creaking doorway at Dover Castle?

At Dover Castle in Kent, the opening and shutting sounds of a creaking doorway are said to be heard. Strangely enough, this happens at a spot where the door no longer stands!

Dover Castle

Windsor Castle

How did Cubbie Roo s Castle get its name?

Cubbie Roo s Castle got its name from the folktale of Giant Cubbie Roo, famous in the Orkney Islands in Scotland. It was one of the earliest Scottish stone castles.

Why is Penhow Castle considered special?

Penhow Castle is the oldest inhabited castle in Wales. Sir William St. Maur built it in the early 13th century.

Which was one of the first castles made for defence against weapons?

Ravenscraig Castle in Scotland was one of the first castles to be made for defence aginst weapons. ¯Built in 1460, it is now partly ruined.

What is the name of the biggest castle in Wales?

The largest castle in Wales is Caerphilly Castle. It was built by Gilbert de Clare between 1268 and 1271, and covers about 121,405 square metres of land.

What makes Chepstow Castle unique?

Dating back to 1067, Chepstow Castle in Wales was one of the first stone castles to be made in Britain. The castle, however, is now in ruins.

What is special about Dover Castle in Kent, England?

One of the largest British castles, Dover Castle is also one of the first to have a circular design. It is known as the Key of England.

Which is the largest castle ruin in England?

Kenilworth Castle in Warwickshire is the largest castle ruin in England. A lake, which ran all the way around the structure, no longer exists.

Which is the biggest castle in England?

The biggest castle in England is Windsor Castle, one of the three homes of the Queen of England. It is said to be the largest inhabited fortress in the world.

Which was the first castle to be built by Edward I?

Flint Castle in Wales was the first castle to be built by Edward I. It was built between 1277 and 1280.

What makes Traquair Castle special?

Built in 1492, Traquair Castle is the oldest home in Scotland. As many as 27 kings have stayed there! The word traquair means a dwelling on a winding stream .

Caerphilly Castle

castles of england

Arundel Castle

Why is Arundel Castle well known to cricket enthusiasts?
Arundel Castle in West Sussex has a cricket ground where many international and county matches are played.

Where can one find Queen Mary s Doll House?
The Doll House at Windsor Castle is a miniature house made during 1921-24. Regarded as one of the most amazing doll houses in the world, it has running water, electricity and working elevators!

What can be found in Dover Castle s wartime tunnels?
Dover Castle s secret tunnel network, which was used during World War II, contains an underground hospital, living spaces, telephone exchanges and war campaign rooms.

What is displayed at Corfe Castle s Plukenet Tower?
Constable Alan de Plukenet s coat-of-arms, or uniform, dating back to the 13th century, is on display at Corfe Castle s Plukenet Tower, in Dorset.

What is unique about the Banqueting Hall at Castle Hedingham?
Castle Hedingham s Banqueting Hall has one of the largest Norman arches in England. It measures about 8.5 metres (27.89 feet).

Which royal castle has the world s largest cut diamond?
The world s largest cut diamond, the Cullinan, or the Great Star of Africa, is part of the British crown jewels at the Tower of London.

What can be seen at Warwick Castle dungeons?
One of the best medieval castles in England, Warwick Castle has a prisoner s message, dating back to the Civil War (1642-51), written on a dungeon wall.

Which is said to be the most haunted castle in England?
12th century Chillingham Castle is said to be the most haunted castle in England.

Who brought the first Christmas tree to Windsor Castle?
Prince Albert, the ˆˆhusband of Queen Victoria, brought the first Christmas tree to Windsor Castle ˆˆin 1834.

What is the importance of the ravens at the Tower of London?
Ravens (large black birds) are kept in the Tower of London because it is believed that the British monarchy will face disaster if the ravens fly away from the tower!

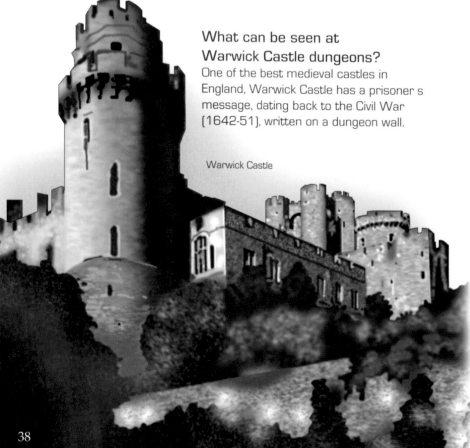

Warwick Castle

Bodium
Castle

Which English castle is commonly known as the fairytale castle?

Bodiam Castle in East Sussex is commonly known as the fairytale castle. Surrounded by a wide moat, it looks as if it is floating on water. The 14th century castle had about 33 fireplaces, 10 spiral staircases and some 28 latrine chutes!

Which castle in England is believed to be King Arthur s birthplace?

In his book History of the Kings of Britain (1136), Geoffrey of Monmouth wrote that King Arthur was born on the grounds of Tintagel Castle in Cornwall.

Which castle is also the oldest brick building in England?

Herstmonceux Castle in East Sussex is the oldest brick structure in England to be still standing. It is surrounded by a wide moat.

What does Deal Castle look like?

Deal Castle is in the shape of a rose with six petals. It was built in Kent during the Tudor period.

What are the popular attractions at Chillingham Castle?

The popular attractions at Chillingham Castle, in Northumberland, include the dungeons, the torture chamber and the room of King Edward I.

Which castle in Suffolk is known for having 13 towers?

12th century Framlingham Castle originally had 13 towers connected by a curtain wall.

Why was Lympne Castle important during the Second World War?

Lympne Castle in Kent served as a major observation post during the Second World War.

Why is Eynsford Castle in Dartford, Kent, unusual?

Built during the 11th century, Eynsford Castle is one of the earliest stone castles in England. After a fire in 1250, the hall was rebuilt and extended into a manor house, which is now in ruins.

What was Guilford Castle converted into?

In 1885, the Guildford Borough Council turned Guilford Castle into a park after the palace buildings were ruined. As the only royal castle in Surrey, it was earlier the centre for governance.

What happened to Bamburgh Castle during the Civil War?

Bamburgh Castle in Northumberland was one of the first castles to be destroyed by cannon firing during the Civil War. Restored in the 1900s, the castle contains many attractions such as archaeology and aviation museums.

Bamburgh Castle

castles of wales

The Carew Cross

Where can the Carew Cross be found?
The Carew Cross, made during the 11th century, guards the entrance of Carew Castle. It is one of the only three early Christian landmarks in Wales, the other two being at Nevern and Maen Achwyfan.

What has Hay Castle been converted into?
A local bookseller in Hay village has turned Hay Castle into a bookshop! Besides book stands inside the castle, there are stalls in the courtyard with a coin box to put the money into.

What is special about the rooms at Cardiff Castle?
At Cardiff Castle in Wales, each room is decorated in a specific theme, including the nursery, the Arab room, or the bedroom with 189 mirrors on the ceiling.

In which castle was the first-ever Prince of Wales born?
The first Prince of Wales, Edward II, was born in the Eagle Tower of Caernarfon Castle, in 1283.

Which musical instrument is the shape of Conwy Castle based upon?
The layout of Conwy Castle is based upon the shape of the Welsh harp.

What was Beaumaris Castle named after?
Beaumaris Castle was given the Norman-French name of Beau Mareys, meaning beautiful marsh. Begun in 1295, its construction was not completed because the builders ran out of money and supplies.

What are the three castles ?
The Grosmont, Skenfrith and White castles were a set of three castles built to protect a route along the border of England and South Wales.

From where did Castell Coch get its name?
Castell Coch means red castle in the Welsh language. In 1875, the castle began to be constructed on the site of the medieval Red Castle s ruins. The walls of the castle are painted with themes from Aesop s Fables.

What is Wogan Cavern?
The Wogan is a natural cave over which Pembroke Castle is built. One can go down into this cavern by a spiral staircase. Flint tools, believed to have been used during the Stone Age, were found there.

From which material is the Great Tower at Raglan Castle made?
The Great Tower at Raglan Castle, in Monmouthshire, is also called the Yellow Tower of Gwent. This is because it is made from yellow sandstone.

Raglan Castle

Why is the space between the towers at Huntingtower Castle known as the Maiden s Leap ?

One of the daughters of the Earl of Gowrie is believed to have jumped across the two towers at Huntingtower Castle to avoid being found with her lover! She leapt across to her own tower when her mother came to check on her.

What was dug out at Carlisle Castle in 2002?

A 1st century tunny fish paste was found in a labelled food jar at Carlisle Castle. This Roman dish was made with tuna fish, dates, honey, vinegar, spices and herbs, to be served with hard-boiled eggs!

Where in Scotland is Inverlochy Castle located?

Inverlochy Castle is situated on the foothills of Ben Nevis, Scotland s highest mountain.

What was recently discovered at a small Ayrshire castle in Scotland?

In July 2002, a rare copy of Jane Austen s novel, Pride and Prejudice, was found at an Ayrshire castle in Scotland. The three-volume set was found in parts in the castle s tower, library and hallway!

How was Dunrobin Castle used during World War I and in the late 1960s?

Scotland s Dunrobin Castle was used as a navy hospital during World War I and as a boys hostel during 1965-72.

Which famous personalities recently got married at Skibo Castle?

Singer Madonna and film director Guy Ritchie held their wedding at the Scottish Skibo Castle. The cost was reportedly about £1.5 million!

Skibo Castle

What is Dirleton Castle known for?

The shrub border at the gardens of Dirleton Castle is believed to be the longest in the world.

What is the One O Clock Gun at Edinburgh Castle?

The One O Clock Gun at Edinburgh Castle is fired everyday at 1.00 p.m. This was begun in 1861 to signal the time to ships in Leith Harbour.

On which television show did Balgonie Castle appear?

In August 2001, the Scottish Balgonie Castle featured on the American TV show, Scariest Places on Earth.

What is special about Ballindalloch Castle?

Ballindalloch Castle is home to the world s oldest herd of the Aberdeen Angus breed of cattle. It was founded in 1860 by Sir George Macpherson-Grant.

Dunrobin Castle

Queen s bathroom at Leeds Castle

What did the bathroom at Leeds Castle look like in the 13th century?

In 1291, the bathroom at Leeds Castle was a stone chamber that was supplied with water from the nearby lake. There was also a shelf for supplies, a place for bathing and a changing room.

Who were minstrels and what did they do at castles?

Minstrels were travelling musicians who sang, played instruments and entertained at castle feasts. Their other important role was to bring news from other towns and castles.

Why are the underground tunnels at Dover Castle historic?

The Dover Castle s tunnels, first dug in 1216, were the largest to be built during the Napoleonic Wars. During World War II, Winston Churchill is said to have planned attacks against the enemy from these tunnels.

What is special about Lincoln Castle?

Lincoln Castle was built by pulling down 166 houses! The castle also contains one of the only four remaining original copies of the Magna Carta, the charter of English liberty.

What is unique about Bridgnorth Castle?

The keep, or tower, at Bridgnorth Castle in England leans at 17 degrees, which is three times more tilted than the Leaning Tower of Pisa!

What was the turning bridge in a castle?

The turning bridge in a castle was an earlier form of the drawbridge and worked like a see-saw.

What was found at Craigmillar Castle in 1813?

A skeleton was found in the walls of Craigmillar Castle in Edinburgh.

What was the role of a castle knight?

Knights were noblemen soldiers who protected the king, queen and other important people in a castle. They had to be trained fighters in order to be able to defend the castle as well as the kingdom.

Which castle is believed to have a hairnet belonging to Mary, Queen of Scots?

Alnwick Castle in Scotland is believed to have a hairnet made from the real hair of Mary, Queen of Scots!

Knight s armour

Why was a knight s armour costly?

A knight s full suit was very expensive as it consisted of about 200 pieces!

Which castle has a splashing water maze?

Hever Castle in Kent has a splashing water maze. The trick is to reach the hollow at the centre without getting wet. If visitors go the wrong way, a splash of water warns them to choose another way!

Water maze at Hever Castle

Which famous personality first lived at Craig Y Nos Castle?

The famous opera singer of the 1800s, Madame Adleina Patti, lived at Craig Y Nos Castle. After she died, this Welsh castle was used as a hospital for about 60 years.

What makes the dining table at Wedderburn Castle special?

In 1897, a 24-seat table was made at Wedderburn Castle, in the dining room itself. Made of oak wood, it has not been removed since.

What was built around the Loudoun Castle ruins?

A theme park was built around the ruins of the 15th century Loudoun Castle. The park has rides with names such as Spiderman, Apollo 2000, Loudoun Leap Log Flume and Ghost Train!

Why is the Chinese Bird Room at Culcreuch Castle unique?

In 1723, the Chinese Bird Room was decorated with hand-painted Chinese wallpaper depicting colourful birds. It is the only place in Scotland to be so decorated.

What is the Smiddy at Ackergill Tower?

The Smiddy at Ackergill Tower, Scotland, was originally used as a place for shoeing horses. It has since been converted into a hotel room for two.

At which castle s dungeon can people eat dinner?

The original dungeon at Dalhousie Castle, in Scotland, has been converted into a cosy restaurant!

Which car race is held at Lincoln Castle every year?

The Lincoln Castle Annual Vintage Car Rally is held every year. Over 200 old cars and trolleys parade the castle grounds then.

What are the Castle Kennedy Horse Driving Trials?

The Castle Kennedy Horse Driving Trials comprise a 3-day horse carriage race that includes a National Carriage Driving Dressage competition and a final race around plastic cones!

Which English castle was used for filming Harry Potter and the Philosopher s Stone ?

The film was shot at Alnwick Castle in Northumberland. This castle, often called the Windsor of the North, has also been a location for films such as Robin Hood and Ivanhoe .

Alnwick Castle